DATE DUE FOR RETURN

D0120366

LV 35874716

LIVERPOOL LIBRARIES

10
LITTLE CIRCUS MICE

by Caroline Stills

illustrated by Judith Rossell

LITTLE HARE
www.littleharebooks.com

For the group I can count on: the Lazy River Writers — CS
For Amber — JR

LIVERPOOL LIBRARIES

3587471

Bertrams | 27/03/2013
| £10.99
SK |

Little Hare Books
an imprint of
Hardie Grant Egmont
Ground Floor, Building 1, 658 Church Street
Richmond, Victoria 3121, Australia

www.littleharebooks.com

Text copyright © Caroline Stills 2013
Illustrations copyright © Judith Rossell 2013

First published 2013

All rights reserved. No part of this publication may be reproduced,
stored in a retrieval system or transmitted in any form or by any means,
electronic, mechanical,photocopying, recording or otherwise, without the prior
written permission of the publisher.

Cataloguing-in-Publication details are available from the National Library of Australia

978 1 921 894 176 (hbk.)

Designed by Vida & Luke Kelly
Produced by Pica Digital, Singapore
Printed through Phoenix Offset
Printed in Shen Zhen, Guangdong Province, China, November 2012

5 4 3 2 1

The illustrations in this book were created with pencil, liquid acrylic and collage.

10 mice wake.

9 mice tidy.

 **1** mouse somersaults.

8 mice cook.

2 mice juggle.

7 mice wash.

3 mice spin.

6 mice peg.

4 mice balance.

5 mice fold.

5 mice clown.

4 mice scrub.

6 mice dive.

3 mice mop.

7 mice totter.

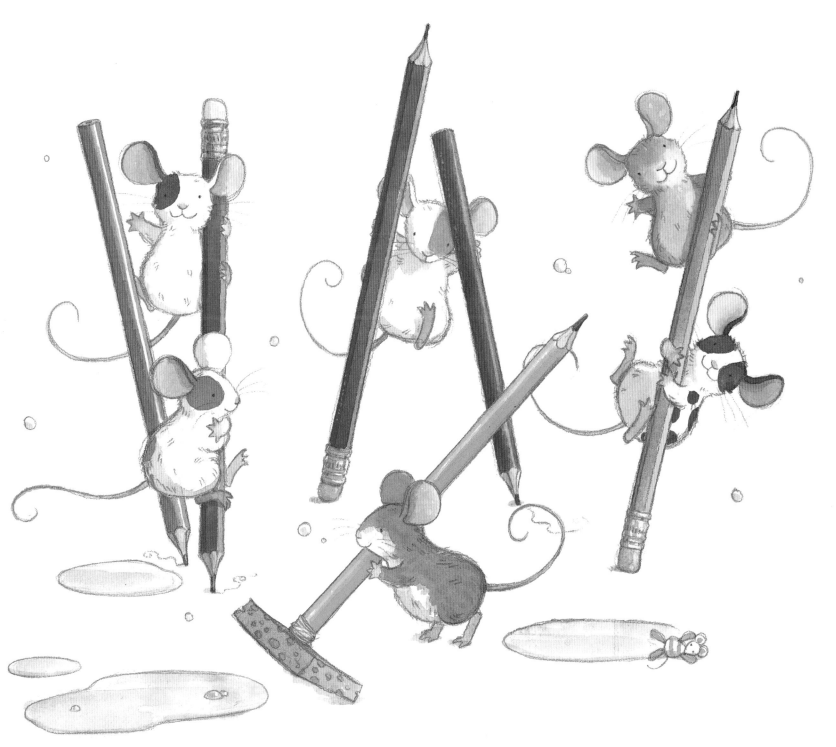

2 mice dust.

8 mice build.

1 mouse polishes.

9 mice swing.

10 mice play.